THE LAST VAMPIRE
AND OTHER STORIES

Bill Peace

MERLIN BOOKS LTD.
Braunton   **Devon**

ISBN 0 86303 435-7
Printed in England by Maslands Ltd., Tiverton, Devon.

CONTENTS

IDENTITY PARADE

John left the tobacconist's with his cigarettes. He always bought his cigarettes at the same shop because this was the only shop that sold French cigarettes. Cigarettes made of dark tobacco.

His friends always complained about the smell but John always said, "Look, I'm smoking them, not you."

John walked to the traffic-lights. He waited for them to change to green.

"Excuse me, sir." John looked round. There was a man in a dark suit. The man continued, "I'm a police-officer and I need your assistance. Can you help me, please?"

"Just a minute. How do I know that you're a police-officer?" asked John.

"Here's my card, sir."

John looked at the card. It seemed genuine.

"How can I help you?" asked John.

"Well, sir, if you don't mind, we need you for an identity parade."

"How long is it going to take?" asked John.

"Not very long, sir. Can you help us?"

"Oh, all right. I've got nothing else to do."

John stood at the end of a line of six men. They were all similar, all about thirty, quite tall with fair hair. Another man was brought in. He was the suspect.

"Stand in the middle," said the officer. The man went to stand in the middle of the line.

Everyone waited. Then the door opened and a policewoman came in with a middle-aged woman. The woman looked a little frightened.

The policewoman brought her close to the line of men. The woman looked at each man carefully. All the men held their breath: they were nervous. The woman reached the end of the line and came back again. She looked at John for a long time.

She went back to the policewoman and whispered something in her ear. The policewoman looked at John, then she took the woman out.

Two policemen appeared. One escorted the suspect out of the room.

"Thank you, gentlemen," said the other officer. "You can go now."

All the men sighed with relief and went towards the door.

"Not you, sir." The officer spoke to John. "Would you like to come to my office?"

They were in the Chief Inspector's office now. The Chief Inspector sat behind his desk. Two other policemen stood at the door. They watched John carefully.

"Now, sir, where were you at one o'clock this afternoon?" asked the inspector.

"What is this?" demanded John.

"Just a few routine questions," replied the inspector calmly. "You see, that woman has identified you."

"Identified me!" exclaimed John.

"Yes. She was in the park and a man came and sat down on the bench beside her. He asked her if he could borrow her paper. When she handed it to him, he pulled the ring off her finger and ran away. She said you were that man."

"But that's ridiculous!" exclaimed John. "I wasn't even in the park."

"Well, sir. We have to make a few inquiries. That's all. Where were you at one o'clock?"

John thought for a moment.

"I'm not sure," he said.

"You mean you don't remember where you were?" asked the inspector.

"Well, I'm trying to remember," said John.

"Were you alone?" asked the inspector.

"Yes, I was alone." He thought for a moment. "I can't remember the exact time but I went to The Red Dragon about lunch-time."

"Did you speak to anybody?"

"Well, I spoke to the barman, but I don't think I spoke to anybody else. I just had a couple of pints."

"And this was about one o'clock?" asked the inspector.

"Yes, I think so."

The inspector nodded to one of the policemen. He left the room and about fifteen minutes later returned with the barman of The Red Dragon.

"I'm sorry to trouble you, sir," said the inspector to the barman, "but can you identify this gentleman? He says he was in your bar around one o'clock and you served him."

The barman looked at John.

"I'm sorry but I don't remember you," he said.

He turned and spoke to the inspector. "I'm not saying he wasn't in my bar. I'm just saying I don't remember him. You see, the bar was full."

"Well, thank you for your help, sir," said the inspector.

The barman went out and the inspector became more serious. He looked at John for a long time. John felt very uncomfortable.

"Can you empty your pockets, please?"

John emptied his pockets. He put the things on the inspector's desk: a key, a packet of cigarettes, a cigarette-lighter, a few banknotes, some loose change, a handkerchief and a ring.

The inspector picked the ring up.

"Where did you get this?" he asked.

"At a second-hand shop in the High Street."

"Where's the receipt?"

"I don't know. I thought it was in my pocket," replied John. He was worried now.

The inspector nodded to one of the policemen at the door. He went out and came back with the middle-aged lady a few minutes later.

"Now, Mrs Smith," he said to the woman. "Can you identify this ring?"

She examined the ring carefully.

"It's mine!" she exclaimed.

"Are you sure?" asked the inspector.

"Well, I think it is. If it isn't, it's very similar," she said.

"And this is the man who took it from you?" asked the inspector.

The woman looked at John. She was very nervous. So was John.

"It's all right, Mrs Smith, don't be afraid," said the inspector.

"Well, I think he's the man, but I'm not certain. You see everything happened so quickly. I don't want to accuse an innocent man."

"Of course not," agreed the inspector.

One of the policemen whispered something in the inspector's ear. The inspector looked at John's packet of cigarettes and nodded.

"Just another couple of questions, Mrs Smith," he said.

"Earlier you said that the man in the park was smoking a cigarette." Mrs Smith nodded.

"Why do you remember that?" asked the inspector.

"Because of the strange smell," she replied.

"You mean it didn't smell like an ordinary cigarette?"

"No, it smelled a lot stronger," she said.

The inspector smiled at her again.

"Now, I'm going to ask you to do something. Don't be afraid. Everything's going to be all right." He picked up John's packet of cigarettes, took one out and gave it to John.

"Smoke this, please," he said. John lit his cigarette and smoked it.

"It's the the same smell," cried Mrs Smith. She was almost hysterical now.

"It's all right, Mrs Smith," said one of the policemen. "Come on, you need a nice cup of tea." He led her out of the door.

"Well," said the inspector to John gravely, "you're in serious trouble."

"But . . . but I've already told you. I didn't steal the ring.

It's my ring. I bought it for my girl-friend."

"Tell me again. Where did you get it?"

"I got it at the second-hand shop in the High Street. The one next to the newsagent's. I saw it in the shop window and went in to buy it." The sweat dripped from John's forehead.

The inspector nodded to the police-officer by the door. He went out of the room.

The inspector asked John a lot of questions. John tried to answer them. The inspector asked the same questions later again. He wanted to confuse John. John was confused.

"I told you, I didn't steal the ring," John cried. "Why don't you believe me?"

Just then, the door opened and a policeman came in with the jeweller of the second-hand shop.

"Thank you for coming, sir," said the inspector.

"What's all this about?" asked the jeweller.

"Well, sir, I'd like to ask you a few questions," said the inspector. "Do you recognize this man?"

"Yes, I do. He bought a ring from me this morning and he forgot his receipt. Here it is."

John sighed with relief.

"And what time was this, sir?"

"Just before one o'clock. This gentleman was my last customer before I closed for lunch."

"I see. Well, thank you very much for your help, sir."

"Not at all, inspector," and the jeweller went out of the office.

The inspector's attitude towards John changed.

"Well, sir. I'm glad to say that you're free to go."

"So am I," replied John.

John walked out of the police station a free man. He walked down the street and stopped at the traffic-lights. He put his hand in his pocket and took out the packet of cigarettes. But instead of lighting one, he threw the packet into the litter-bin.

"I'm not going to smoke any more. It's not worth the trouble."

"DON'T DRINK AND DRIVE"

It was Wednesday night. Christine and Julie were having a drink in the Black Bull. It was the girls' night out. The one night of the week when they went out without their husbands.

"Do you know that man over there?" asked Julie.

"Which one?" asked Christine.

"The one with the bald head, wearing a brown jacket."

Christine looked over to the bar. There was a middle-aged man with a bald head, standing by himself.

"No. I've never seen him before," said Christine. "Why?"

"Well, he keeps looking at us."

Christine looked at the man again. Just then the man turned his head and looked at Christine. Their eyes met. Christine looked away.

"Don't look at him," she said to Julie. "I think he's drunk. We don't want him to come over here."

The two women started talking about other things. But they felt uncomfortable because the man kept looking at them.

"Finish your drink and let's go," said Christine after a few minutes. "I don't like that man looking at us."

Julie finished her drink and the two women got up to go. As they were going towards the door, the man was looking at them. He spoke to them but they ignored him.

The two women went out of the pub and walked towards the car. Julie looked over her shoulder and saw the man. He was standing in the pub doorway.

"That man's come out of the pub," she said. "I think he's following us."

"Come on, then. Let's get out of here," said Christine.

The two women got quickly into the car and Christine

started the engine. Julie, who was in the passenger seat, looked out of the window.

"He's coming over here," she said nervously.

But by this time, the car was by the car-park exit. Christine drove slowly out of the car-park and turned left into the main road.

"We're all right now," said Christine.

"No, we're not," said Julie. "He's running after us."

Christine looked in the driver's mirror. She could see the man, running in the middle of the road.

"Oh, my God!" exclaimed Julie. "The traffic-lights! We've got to stop at the lights."

The traffic-lights were twenty metres ahead and they were red. Christine drove up to the lights and stopped the car.

"Lock the door," she said.

Julie obeyed her and then looked round. She could see the man through the back window of the car. He was about ten metres away now.

The traffic-lights showed red and amber. Christine was ready to go. But the man was by the car. He tried to open the door but it was locked. Just then, the traffic-lights changed to green and the car moved away.

"Stop," shouted the man. And he hit the side of the car with his hand.

Julie looked round. She saw the man through the back window. He was standing in the middle of the road, looking at the car.

When Christine got home, she told her husband, Phillip, about the man. But Phillip was more interested in the football match on television.

"He was probably drunk. Forget it," was all Phillip said.

About two weeks later, Phillip and Christine decided to go out for a drink. They went to the Black Bull.

While they were having a drink, Christine noticed the man by the bar. He was standing by himself.

"Phillip, you see that man over there? The one wearing the brown jacket."

Phillip looked at the man. He was a middle-aged man with a bald head.

"What about him?" asked Phillip.

"He's the man who followed Julie and me the other week."

"Are you sure?" asked Phillip.

"Well, I think so," replied Christine.

Just then the man looked at Phillip. Their eyes met for a second, and then Phillip looked away.

"Don't worry about him," said Phillip. "He's an old man."

A few minutes later, Phillip and Christine finished their drinks and left the pub. While they were walking towards the car, Christine heard the pub door open. She turned round and saw the man in the doorway.

"It's that man again," she said. "He's following us."

"I don't think so," said Phillip. "He's probably going home. That's all."

They were by the car now. Phillip had the car key in his hand. He was about to open the door when the man spoke to him.

"Excuse me," said the man. "I hope you're not going to drive."

"What do you mean?" said Phillip.

"I mean what I say," replied the man. "I hope you're not going to drive."

"Why not?" asked Phillip.

"Because you've been drinking," said the man.

Phillip realized that the man was drunk and he did not want an argument. He opened the car door.

"Get in, Christine," he said. But before Christine could get into the car, the man pushed the door shut.

"Now, just watch it," said Phillip angrily.

The man put his hand on Phillip's shoulder. "Look. I'm telling you. Don't drive. You've been drinking."

Phillip pushed the man's hand from his shoulder. He spoke to the man angrily.

"Listen to me. It's none of your business. Now go away and

leave us alone."

He spoke to Christine. "Get in the car and let's go."

Christine got into the car. But before Phillip could open the other door, the man grabbed Phillip's arm.

"You're not going to drive," said the man. "You've been drinking."

Phillip pushed the man away and opened the door. But the man grabbed him by the shirt.

"Take your hands off me!" shouted Phillip. He pushed the man in the chest and the man fell to the ground.

Phillip got quickly into the car and started the engine.

"Are you all right?" asked Christine.

"Yes, I'm OK," replied Phillip. "My shirt's torn. That's all."

Phillip switched on the headlights and started driving towards the car-park gates.

Suddenly there was the sound of breaking glass.

"Oh, my God!" exclaimed Christine. "The stupid man has broken the back window."

Phillip was furious. He stopped the car and was about to get out.

"Don't get out, Phillip. We don't want any more trouble. Let's go to the police," suggested Christine.

"Yes. That's a good idea," agreed Phillip.

Phillip ignored the shouting man and drove out of the car-park.

Five minutes later Phillip and Christine were in the police station.

Phillip explained what had happened in the pub car-park. And Christine also told the police-officer about her experience with the man.

"And you say that the man was middle-aged," said the officer.

"Yes, and he was . . . ."

"He was bald, and he was wearing a brown jacket," interrupted the officer.

"Well, yes. But how do you know that?" asked Phillip,

surprised.

"Well, let me explain," replied the officer. "During the past year, several people have complained about this man, Joe Hodge. The people all told the same, or a similar story. Joe had argued with them outside the Black Bull. Sometimes he had become violent and had hit people or broken a car window."

"But why?" asked Phillip.

"Well," replied the officer. "About a year ago Joe's daughter, Sandra, went to the Black Bull. She had several drinks and got drunk. Then, when she was driving home, her car crashed into a tree. Sandra was taken to hospital, but died a few hours later."

"That's terrible," said Christine.

"Yes, it is," agreed Phillip. "Now I understand why he didn't want me to drive. But he can't break car windows or attack people. It's not right. Why don't you arrest him?"

"We can't do that," replied the officer. "You see, two weeks after his daughter's death, Joe Hodge died of a broken heart."

THE BOXER

The calendar on the gymnasium wall said Monday 6 July. Jack Blackburn was watching the two boxers carefully.

"OK boys," he said after a few minutes. "That's enough for today. Now go and have a shower."

The two sweating men climbed out of the boxing ring and went towards the changing room.

"Joe," said Blackburn.

The big, fair-haired boxer turned round.

"I want to see you before you go."

"All right, Mr Blackburn," said Joe.

Twenty minutes later, Joe came out of the changing room. He walked across the gymnasium and knocked at the door of the small office in the corner.

"Come in, Joe," said the voice from inside.

Joe opened the door and went in. Jack Blackburn was sitting at the table.

"Sit down, Joe," said Blackburn.

Joe sat down.

"Well, how do you feel?" asked Blackburn.

"I feel good. Really good," replied Joe.

"I know you do," said Blackburn. "You're in perfect condition." Blackburn sat back in his chair and looked at the poster on the wall.

HEAVYWEIGHT CHAMPIONSHIP FIGHT
JOE JARRETT v KARL COOPER
THURSDAY 9 JULY

Blackburn said nothing for a few seconds. Then he spoke.

"You know something, Joe. I've waited twenty-five years for this. I've been a trainer for twenty-five years. Did you know that?"

Joe said nothing so Blackburn continued. "I've trained a lot of good boxers in my time, but you're the best."

Blackburn looked again at the poster on the wall.

"Karl Cooper," he continued, "is a good boxer. But he's not in your class. You can beat him, Joe."

"I'll beat him, Mr Blackburn," said Joe.

"I know you will," said Blackburn.

"What are the plans from now until Thursday?" asked Joe.

Blackburn explained what he wanted Joe to do.

"From now on, I just want you to do some light training. That's all. I want you to be in bed by ten o'clock every night. Remember, a good night's sleep is very important. Then go for a run every morning. About fifteen miles. After that, have a light breakfast. Then I'll see you in the gymnasium at eleven o'clock. OK?"

"OK Mr Blackburn."

Joe walked out of the gymnasium. Jack Blackburn watched him and thought: 'Joe's the best boy I've ever had. And on Thursday night he'll be the new heavyweight champion.'

Joe went home and watched television all afternoon. In the evening, he thought to himself: 'I think I'll go round to the discotheque and see my brother.'

Joe left the house and walked round to the discotheque. It was not far. About a ten minutes' walk. He did not have to pay to get in because his brother was one of the barmen.

"Hey, Joe. What are you having? A double whisky?" joked his brother, Tom.

"Just give me an orange juice," said Joe.

The two brothers stood talking for some time. Then Tom moved down the bar to serve some people.

Joe looked over to the dance floor. The lights were dim and several couples were dancing to the rhythm of the music. Other people were sitting at the tables around the dance floor.

Just then a woman got up from one of the tables. She

walked quickly towards the exit. But a man followed her and caught her by the arm.

"Let go of me!" said the woman, turning round.

"I won't," said the man. "You're my girl-friend and you're staying with me."

Joe heard all of this because the two people were standing right in front of him.

The woman pushed the man's arm away and started walking towards the door. But the man took her arm again and started pulling her towards the dance floor. The woman struggled but the man was too strong for her. She started crying.

At this point, Joe decided to do something.

"Just a minute," he said to the man.

The man turned and looked at Joe.

"Stay out of this," the man said. "It's none of your business."

Joe hesitated. The man was right. It was none of his business. But the woman was crying.

"Are you all right?" Joe asked the woman.

The man let go of the woman's arm. He turned to face Joe.

"Look. I've just told you. Stay out of this." And he pushed Joe in the chest.

Joe did nothing. It was not necessary. Two of the barmen had seen everything. They caught the man by the arms and took him outside.

Joe and the woman were left alone.

"Are you all right?" asked Joe.

"Yes, I'm OK," replied the woman. "Thank you for helping me."

"Can I get you anything?" asked Joe.

"No, thank you. I just want to go home. Thanks again for your help."

The woman went out of the dance-hall and into the ladies' cloakroom. When she came out, five minutes later, Joe was waiting for her.

"Are you sure you'll be all right?" he asked.

"Well, I am a little frightened. Bob may be waiting outside."

"Come on, then. I'll take you home," said Joe.

"Are you sure?" asked the woman. "I don't want to spoil your night."

"It's OK, I was going anyway," replied Joe.

Joe and the woman — her name was Josephine — left the discotheque. The man, Bob, was not waiting outside.

As they were walking towards Josephine's flat, Joe said, "Do you want to tell me about it?"

"There's nothing to tell, really. I've been out with Bob three or four times. That's all. But he thinks he owns me."

Five minutes later, they were at Josephine's flat.

"Would you like to come inside?" she asked.

Joe looked at his watch. 10.15.

"Well, I . . . . Oh, all right. Just for a little while."

Josephine showed Joe into the flat. She explained that she shared the flat with another girl. Her girl-friend had gone away for a few days.

"What can I get you to drink?" asked Josephine. "I'm going to have a whisky."

"Have you got any orange juice?"

"What's the matter? Don't you drink?"

Joe did not want to explain that he was in training. He just smiled.

"Come on," said Josephine, smiling back. "Have a whisky with me."

"Well, all right. But just a little one. With plenty of ice."

Josephine filled two glasses with whisky and sat down on the sofa next to Joe.

The music was soft and romantic. The lights were dim. Josephine had her head on Joe's shoulder. Her hair felt soft. He could smell her perfume.

Joe opened his eyes. He saw the whisky bottle on the table. Half empty! He looked at his watch. 1.30!

"Josephine," he whispered.

Josephine moved her head slightly.

"Josephine," whispered Joe again. "It's late. I have to go."

Josephine did not move. She kept her head on Joe's shoulder.

"Don't go," she said. "It's so nice like this."

"I have to," said Joe.

Joe moved Josephine's head from his shoulder and stood up. He looked down at the girl, who was now lying on the sofa. She was very pretty, with blonde hair.

"Why won't you stay, Joe?" she asked.

"Because I have to be up very early in the morning," he replied.

Before Joe left, he arranged to ring Josephine the following evening.

Fifteen minutes later, Joe was at home. The time was 1.45. He set the alarm-clock for 7 o'clock and got into bed. He fell asleep immediately.

Two minutes later, it seemed, he was woken by a noise. What was it? "Ring, ring . . . ring, ring . . . ring, ring." It was the alarm-clock ringing. It was 7 o'clock.

Joe sat up in bed.

'Oh, my head,' he thought. He had a terrible headache.

He got out of bed slowly and went to the bathroom. The cold shower made him feel better. He dried himself quickly and got into his tracksuit. He was ready for his morning run.

He ran through the streets to the end of the town. Then he was running towards the country. He started running quickly, but after a few minutes he slowed down. His legs were aching. He did not want to go on, but he had to. He had to run for at least two hours.

He went on running slowly for another twenty minutes. But it was hard. Very hard.

'This is no good. I don't feel like running today,' he thought. He turned round and ran slowly back home. When he got home, he had another shower. Then he went back to bed. But he could not sleep. He lay in bed thinking. Thinking about Josephine. Thinking about the fight on Thursday night.

He got out of bed at half-past ten and went to the

gymnasium.

Jack Blackburn was already there.

"Get changed and get in the ring, Joe," Blackburn said. "I want you to box a few rounds with a lightweight."

A few minutes later, the two boxers came out of the changing room and got into the ring — Joe, the big, blond heavyweight and the much smaller man. Blackburn spoke to both men.

"OK, Johnny. I want you to run and dance as much as possible. And Joe, I want to see how fast you are."

Jack Blackburn watched the two boxers in the ring. They boxed a few rounds and then Blackburn told them to stop.

"What's the matter, Joe?" he asked. "You looked tired."

"I'm all right. I didn't sleep too well. That's all," said Joe.

"But you went for your run, didn't you?" asked Blackburn.

"Oh, yes, I ran fifteen miles," lied Joe.

Blackburn seemed satisfied with Joe's explanation.

Joe trained for another hour and then went to have a shower. Before he left the gymnasium, Blackburn said to him: "Remember, Joe. A good night's sleep is the most important thing you can get."

Joe went home and had a big lunch. A large steak, three eggs and lots of vegetables. After his meal, he relaxed and watched television.

He rang Josephine at eight o'clock.

"Hello. It's me, Joe."

"Oh, Joe. I'm glad you've rung. I'm so frightened. Bob's rung three times and he says he's coming round," said Josephine.

Joe thought quickly. "Listen, Josephine. There's nothing to worry about. Just don't open the door."

"But I'm frightened, Joe."

"Don't worry. Everything's going to be all right. I'll come round if you want."

"Please, Joe."

Jose got to Josephine's flat ten minutes later.

"Oh, Joe. I'm glad you've come. Bob's rung again," said

Josephine.

"You've nothing to worry about now," said Joe. "I'm here."

Josephine had already put two glasses on the table. She now filled them with whisky.

"I need this," she said, lifting her glass to her lips.

Joe sat down on the sofa. He did not touch his whisky.

"What's the matter, Joe? Aren't you drinking?" asked Josephine.

Joe explained about himself. He told Josephine that he was a boxer. And he had a very important fight the following Thursday.

Josephine was very surprised.

"I'm sorry, Joe. I had no idea." Then she smiled at him.

"So that's why you didn't stay with me last night. I thought it was because you didn't like me."

Joe put his arms around her.

"I do like you, Josephine. I think you are a wonderful girl."

Just then the phone rang. Josephine picked it up. "Hello," she said. No one spoke. She put the phone down. "Wrong number, I suppose."

They decided to watch the film on television. The film finished at ten o'clock, and then Joe got up to go.

"It's all right, Joe. I understand," said Josephine as she opened the door for him.

Just then the phone rang again. Josephine went over and picked up the receiver.

"Who's there?" she said in a nervous voice. But the person on the other end of the line did not speak.

"That's the second time," she said, looking at Joe. "I think somebody is trying to frighten me."

Joe came back into the room and sat down.

"Do you think it's Bob?" he asked.

"I don't know. I don't know what to think."

Josephine sat down on the sofa beside Joe.

"I feel safe while you're here with me," she said, putting her head on his shoulder.

Joe stayed with Josephine for another two hours. But the telephone did not ring again.

It was 12.30 when Joe got home. He went straight to bed. But he did not set the alarm-clock for 7 o'clock, he set it for 10 o'clock.

The following morning Joe woke up feeling good. He had had nearly ten hours' sleep. He went to the gymnasium.

Jack Blackburn was watching Joe carefully during his training session.

"You're quicker than you were yesterday," said Blackburn.

"Yes, I feel good," replied Joe.

"And how was your run?" asked Blackburn.

"Oh, I ran for over two hours," lied Joe.

"That's good," said Blackburn. "Now go home and take it easy. Just relax. Read a book or something. Tomorrow's the big day. Remember, to be in perfect condition, you need at least twelve hours' sleep."

"I'll do that, Mr Blackburn," Joe promised.

Joe had not arranged to see Josephine that evening. She knew that the following day was the most important in his life. And she also knew that he needed as much rest as possible.

She rang him at 7 o'clock to ask how he was. Joe told her that he felt good. And he was about to go to bed.

Joe was woken up at midnight by the telephone. He picked it up.

"Joe," said the voice. It was Josephine. She sounded very frightened.

"What's the matter?" said Joe.

Josephine said that her telephone had rung several times. Each time she picked it up, nobody spoke. All she could hear was heavy breathing. Somebody was trying to frighten her.

"Don't worry. Everything's going to be all right. I'll be round in fifteen minutes," said Joe.

When Joe got to Josephine's flat, she still looked a little nervous.

"I'm sorry about this, Joe," she said. "But I was so frightened." She started crying.

"It's all right now," said Joe, putting his arms around her.

The following morning, Joe was woken up when Josephine opened the curtains.

"What time is it?" asked Joe.

"Ten o'clock," was the reply.

Joe groaned. He had only slept for about six hours.

"Come on. Here's your breakfast," she said, putting the breakfast tray in front of him.

After breakfast, Josephine showed Joe the newspaper.

"There's an article about you on the back page," she said.

Joe took the newspaper and read the headlines:

JOE JARRETT WILL WIN

"Do you think you'll win?" asked Josephine.

"I hope so," replied Joe. "Do you want to come to the fight?"

Josephine hesitated before she replied. "No, Joe. I don't like boxing. I'm afraid of violence."

"Josephine," Joe began, "if I win tonight, I'll be the champion." He stopped because it was difficult to say what he wanted to say.

"Er . . . er . . . I've only known you for two or three days but I . . . er . . . "

"Yes, Joe?"

"Will you marry me, Josephine?"

Josephine looked at Joe seriously. "Joe, I . . . I don't know what to say. We haven't known each other long enough."

"But you do love me, don't you?" asked Joe.

"Yes, Joe. I love you."

Joe smiled and put his arms around her.

"Then we can talk about it after the fight. As soon as the fight is over, I'll phone you."

That evening Joe met Jack Blackburn in the gymnasium. From there they went by taxi to the Palace Sports Centre. Hundreds of people were standing outside, but Joe and Blackburn went in by the back door.

At 8 o'clock the hall was full of people. Everyone cheered when the two boxers climbed into the ring.

The referee spoke to the two boxers: "Remember, I want a good, clean fight. Do you understand, Joe? Do you understand, Karl?"

Both boxers nodded in agreement.

"Now shake hands," said the referee. "And when the bell rings, come out fighting."

The two boxers shook hands and then went back to their corners.

The bell rang, and Karl rushed over to Joe's corner and hit Joe in the face. Karl tried to hit Joe again but Joe backed away. Joe moved to his left and then moved forward. He tried to hit Karl but Karl moved away quickly.

The fight was long and hard. Sometimes Joe hit Karl and sometimes Karl hit Joe. But Joe was getting very tired. It was difficult to move his legs. He wanted to stop. But he had to go on.

The two fighters came out for round fifteen, the last round. Joe moved forward and tried to hit Karl. But Karl was too quick for him. He hit Joe in the face. Once, twice, three times.

Joe went down. The referee started counting: "One . . . two . . . three . . ."

"Get up, Joe," shouted Blackburn.

"Four . . . five . . . six . . ."

Joe tried to get up but he fell down again.

"Seven . . . eight . . . nine . . . ten!"

The fight was over. Karl Cooper was the new Heavyweight Champion. The crowd clapped and cheered. It had been a good fight.

The champagne party was cancelled. Joe was taken home by taxi.

When he got home, he rang Josephine. But there was no answer. He called her several times but she was not at home.

Joe went to bed and fell asleep immediately.

He woke up late the next day. After his shower, he went downstairs. He picked up the newspaper which was sticking through the letter-box. He sat down and looked at the sports page.

There was a big picture of the new champion, Karl Cooper with his girl-friend. They were going to spend a few weeks in Bermuda, said the newspaper report.

Joe looked and looked again at the photograph. Beside the bruised face of Karl Cooper, there was the happy face of a woman. A pretty woman with blonde hair. She was looking straight into Joe's eyes. And smiling at him in the same way that she had smiled at him two nights ago.

THE LAST VAMPIRE

Doctor Bloodclott was woken up by the telephone. It was 1 a.m.

"Can you come quickly, doctor?" asked the anxious voice. "It's my daughter, Veronica. She's very ill."

"Who is speaking?" asked the doctor.

"It's Major Silversword of the Black Castle."

"Right, Major. I'll be there in fifteen minutes."

Ten minutes later, Dr Bloodclott rang the doorbell of the Black Castle.

The Black Castle was not really a castle. But it was a very big house, over five hundred years old. It was surrounded by a beautiful garden with high trees. Behind the garden, about two hundred metres from the house, was the graveyard. Most of the graves were very old. Some of the bodies there had been buried a long time ago. In the corner of the graveyard, was the chapel. The chapel had not been used for a very long time.

Major Silversword, himself, opened the door.

"Thank you for coming so quickly," he said.

He showed the doctor into Veronica's bedroom. Veronica's mother and her sister, Madeline, were sitting at the bedside.

Dr Bloodclott examined his patient, a girl of nineteen. She was sweating and her temperature was very high.

"She has a fever," said the doctor. "How long has she been like this?"

"About two hours," answered Mrs Silversword.

"Right," said the doctor. "I'm going to give her an injection. It will put her to sleep."

The doctor took a syringe from his bag. He injected the girl in the arm.

The injection worked quickly. Veronica was asleep within

29

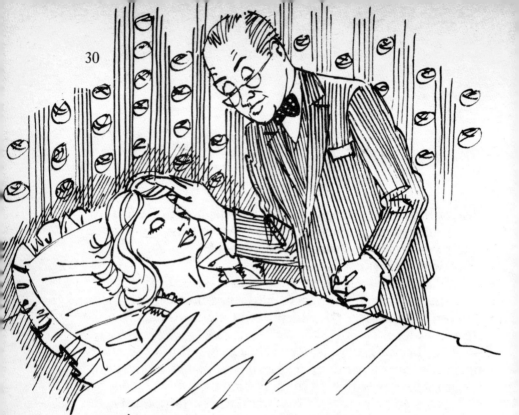

two minutes.

"Will she be all right, doctor?" asked Madeline, a girl of about seventeen.

"Yes, I think so," replied the doctor. "I'll come and see her tomorrow morning."

When Dr Bloodclott came the following day, Veronica was still asleep. Her temperature was normal and she looked very peaceful.

"I'll come back this evening," said the doctor. "I can't really examine her while she is asleep."

When the doctor saw Veronica that evening, he became worried. Veronica was still asleep.

"No, she hasn't woken up at all," said the major, when the doctor asked him.

The doctor did not know what to think. But he had to say something.

"When she wakes up, give her some hot soup," he said. "And I'll come and see her tomorrow."

The following day was the same: Veronica was still unconscious. The doctor felt the girl's pulse. It was very weak.

The others looked at the doctor. They expected him to say something. He had to think quickly.

"I'd like Veronica to have a routine examination. So I'm going to send her to hospital," he said in a professional voice. "But there is nothing to worry about."

Veronica was taken to hospital by ambulance. She was examined by a specialist, Dr Prickitt, who was a friend of Dr Bloodclott's.

"I don't understand this," said Dr Prickitt to Dr Bloodclott. "I can't find anything wrong with this girl. But she's getting weaker all the time."

"Do you think . . . . ?" Dr Bloodclott stopped because he did not want to say the words.

"Yes, I do. I think she's going to die," said Dr Prickitt.

"But isn't there anything we can do?"

"What else can we do? We've tried everything."

Dr Prickitt was right. Veronica died the following day. Her family, who had been at the bedside, were heart-broken.

Veronica's body was taken to the laboratory. There it was examined by Dr Lookall, the pathologist.

After the pathologist's examination, Dr Bloodclott and Dr Prickitt were called to the laboratory.

"I don't know what to think," explained Dr Lookall. "I can't find any cause of death. But come and look at the body."

The three doctors walked over to the table where the body was lying. They looked down at the dead girl. Veronica was very beautiful, with fair hair and a pale skin.

"Look at these," said Dr Lookall. He pointed to two small marks on Veronica's neck.

Dr Prickitt and Dr Bloodclott looked closely.

"I didn't notice these marks before," said Dr Prickitt.

"Neither did I," said Dr Bloodclott.

"Well, they are very small," said Dr Lookall.

"Are the marks important?" asked Dr Bloodclott.

"No, I don't think so. They certainly did not cause her death," said Dr Lookall.

"Then what did cause her death?" asked Dr Bloodclott.

"I don't know. I just don't know," said Dr Lookall.

Dr Lookall showed the other two doctors a paper.

"This is the death certificate. And I've written: 'Death due to natural causes'."

Veronica's funeral took place two days later. She was buried in the graveyard behind the Black Castle. After the funeral, Madeline was sent to Paris.

"I want Madeline to get away from here for a few weeks," said her father.

Madeline came back home two months later. She looked and felt a lot better. She did not talk about Veronica. But she thought about her a lot.

One night, after Madeline had been back home for about two weeks, Major Silversword was woken up. He could hear a noise from the next bedroom. It was Madeline. She was crying.

The major got out of bed and went into his daughter's bedroom. Madeline was sitting up in bed, staring at the window.

"Don't go. Please don't go, Veronica," she sobbed.

Major Silversword put his arms round his daughter.

"It's all right, my dear. It's all right."

"I've just seen Veronica, Daddy. She was here with me."

"You've been dreaming. That's all," said her father.

"No, I haven't, Daddy. I saw her. I really saw her. She was wearing a white night-gown. And she looked so beautiful."

Major Silversword stayed with his daughter until she fell asleep. Then he went back to his own bedroom.

The same thing happened the following night. Major Silversword had to get up to comfort his daughter. Madeline said that she had seen Veronica. And Veronica had kissed her.

The major was very worried, so he phoned Dr Bloodclott the following day. The doctor said that Madeline needed some sleeping tablets.

"They will help her to get a good night's sleep," said the doctor.

That evening Madeline took two sleeping tablets with hot milk before she went to bed. But again, her father was woken up in the middle of the night. When he went into Madeline's bedroom, she was standing by the open window.

"Veronica, Veronica," she was crying.

The major put his daughter back to bed and stayed with her for the rest of the night.

Dr Bloodclott was called the following morning. Madeline was still in bed when the doctor made his visit. He spoke to the major for several minutes. Then he was shown into Madeline's bedroom.

The doctor sat down beside the bed and listened to the young girl. When she had finished, he gave her some advice.

"This is a normal situation, Madeline. What's happening to you, happens to a lot of people."

"But I saw her, Doctor. I wasn't dreaming."

"You only think you saw her," replied the doctor smiling. "Now open your mouth. I'm going to take your temperature."

The doctor put the thermometer into the girl's mouth. As he did this, he noticed something. There were two small marks on the left side of her neck. He looked closely at the marks but said nothing about them.

Madeline's temperature was normal and the doctor said there was nothing physically wrong with her. He left the house after he had given her some different sleeping tablets.

"Take two of these before you go to bed," he said. "And I'm sure you'll have a good night's sleep."

When Dr Bloodclott got home, he phoned Dr Lookall at the hospital. He told him about the marks on Madeline's neck. Dr Lookall was very interested.

"I'd like to examine Madeline," said Dr Lookall.

"But how can you?" asked Dr Bloodclott. "If I take you with me to the house, the family will be very suspicious."

"Then why can't I go instead of you? I can say that you have been called away on an emergency."

Dr Bloodclott thought for a few moments. Then he agreed.

The following day Dr Lookall, instead of Dr Bloodclott, visited Madeline. After his visit, he went immediately to see Dr Bloodclott.

"What do you know about vampires?" asked Dr Lookall.

Dr Bloodclott looked very surprised.

"Vampires! What do you mean?"

"Well," said Dr Lookall seriously. "These marks on Madeline's neck are the same as the marks that were on Veronica's neck. And I think they are the marks of a vampire."

"But vampires don't exist. They have never existed," said Dr Bloodclott.

"I'm not so sure," said Dr Lookall. "I believe vampires did exist until the sixteenth century."

"But we are living in the 1980s. This is absurd," said Dr Bloodclott.

"Look. Let's examine the facts," said Dr Lookall. "A nineteen-year-old girl died. And we could find no cause of death. The girl had two small marks on her neck. Now her sister has two similar marks in the same place."

"I'm not going to listen to this nonsense," said Dr Bloodclott. "There must be a more logical explanation."

Dr Lookall soon left. Now that Dr Bloodclott was alone, he had time to think about what Dr Lookall had said.

That evening, Dr Bloodclott went to see Professor Dateman, a historian.

"What do you know about vampires?" asked Dr Bloodclott.

Professor Dateman was not surprised by the question. He sat back in his chair and looked serious.

"Well, they exist. Or they used to exist until the sixteenth century," he said.

"But what exactly was a vampire?" asked Dr Bloodclott.

"A vampire was the living dead. A person who had not really died."

"What do you mean?"

"Well, when a person dies, his spirit leaves the body. And the body decomposes until only the bones are left.

"But the vampire was different. After death, the spirit stayed in the body. And the body did not decompose. In order to survive, the vampire needed blood. Human blood. Usually the blood of a young woman."

"Why a young woman?" asked Dr Bloodclott.

"Because the blood of a young woman is sweeter. And her skin is softer."

Dr Bloodclott said nothing so the professor continued: "The vampire came out from his grave at night, always at night because the sun was dangerous for him. Then he entered the bedroom of a young woman, bit her neck with his long teeth and sucked her blood. The blood he needed to survive."

"And what happened to the young woman?" asked Dr Bloodclott.

"Well, nothing at first. But after a few weeks, the woman became ill. Then she got a fever and died a few days later."

Dr Bloodclott opened his mouth to speak. But he could not say anything. The professor continued.

"When I say 'died', I don't really mean that. I mean that the woman herself became a vampire."

The professor noticed the strange expression on Dr Bloodclott's face.

"What's the matter? You look frightened."

Dr Bloodclott told him about Veronica and Madeline. The professor listened carefully. Sometimes he asked a question.

When the doctor had finished, the professor said: "And you say that this girl, Madeline, lives in the Black Castle?"

"Yes."

"Then we must do something quickly," said the professor.

The doctor noticed the urgency in the professor's voice.

"What do you know about the Black Castle?" he asked the professor.

"Well, in the sixteenth century, the owner of the Black Castle was a man called Suckchops. Count Suckchops. Counts were very rich and important people in those days, you understand."

The doctor nodded and the professor continued.

"Count Suckchops died in a strange way. Some people said he was murdered. Others said he killed himself. But nobody found out exactly how he died.

"The count was buried in the graveyard behind the Black Castle. Only his two daughters, girls of about eighteen, and the servants attended the funeral.

"After the funeral, the count's daughters did not want to stay in the Black Castle. They said the house was too big for them. So they decided to sell it.

"A man came to the house and wanted to buy it. The two daughters and the man agreed on a price. But before the house was sold, something happened."

"What happened?" asked Dr Bloodclott.

"The elder daughter, Lucinda, started waking up in the middle of the night. She said that her father appeared in her bedroom. He came in through the window."

"Did the others believe her?" asked Dr Bloodclott.

"No. Not at the time. They thought Lucinda was dreaming."

"So what happened?"

"Well, this situation went on for a few weeks. Then Lucinda became very ill and died."

"Really!" said the doctor, looking uncomfortable.

The professor went on: "The younger daughter, Matilda, believed that Lucinda had died of natural causes. She did not believe in vampires. But one night, about a week after Lucinda's death, she woke up.

"There was a noise at the window. Then the window opened and a shadow came in. Matilda was very frightened. She closed her eyes. She thought she was dreaming. But when she opened her eyes again, she saw her father, Count Suckchops. He was standing beside the bed, smiling at her."

"What happened?" asked the doctor.

"Matilda screamed and the servants came running into the

bedroom."

"Did they see Count Suckchops?"

"No. When Matilda screamed, he disappeared through the window."

"So what happened?"

"Well, the servants thought that Matilda had had a nightmare. But Matilda was sure that she had seen her father. And she was sure that her father was a vampire.

"She left the Black Castle the following day and never came back. The servants were given some money and the house was closed down."

"For how long?" asked Dr Bloodclott.

"Until the 1920s. Then Major Silversword's grandfather bought the house."

"You mean nobody lived in the Black Castle for three hundred years?"

"That's right," answered Professor Dateman. "But we are wasting time. We have to do something quickly. If we don't do anything, Madeline will die."

Twenty minutes later, Professor Dateman and Dr Bloodclott were knocking at the door of the Black Castle.

Major Silversword opened the door. He looked very worried.

"I'm glad you've come, doctor, Madeline is very ill," he said.

The three men went upstairs to Madeline's bedroom.

Madeline was asleep. Dr Bloodclott felt her pulse. It was very weak.

"We must get her into hospital immediately," said the doctor. He spoke to Professor Dateman.

"You explain to the major while I phone the hospital."

Dr Bloodclott telephoned the hospital. He arranged for an ambulance to come immediately. When he came back to the bedroom, Major Silversword was looking terrible.

"Vampires!" said the major. "I don't believe it. This is the twentieth century."

"It's true, major. A vampire killed Veronica. And, if we don't get Madeline out of this house, she will die, as well," said the doctor.

The ambulance soon arrived. Madeline was rushed to hospital. She was given a blood transfusion immediately.

In the meantime, Major and Mrs Silversword and the servants left the house. They went to stay with some friends in the village.

Dr Bloodclott and Professor Dateman were alone in the Black Castle.

"There is nothing we can do tonight," said the professor. "Let's go home and have a good night's sleep. Then we can start early in the morning."

The following morning, Professor Dateman met Dr Bloodclott in the grounds of the Black Castle. The professor opened the boot of his car. He took out a thick stick, a wooden hammer and two shovels.

"What's this for?" asked the doctor, looking at the stick. The stick was about three feet long, and it was pointed at one end, like a pencil.

"I'm going to kill the vampires with this stick," said the professor. "We have to put it into the vampires' hearts. Come on. Let's find Veronica's grave."

The two men found Veronica's grave easily. It was the newest in the graveyard.

"Right. Start digging," said the professor. He gave the doctor one of the shovels.

The two men dug for over an hour. It was very hard work. Finally, one of the shovels touched something hard. It was the wooden coffin. Five minutes later, the two men had cleared away all the earth over the coffin. They could see the coffin clearly.

"Climb out of the grave," said the professor.

The doctor climbed out of the grave. He looked down at the professor. Professor Dateman was standing with his feet on either side of the coffin.

The professor hit the side of the coffin several times with his shovel. Then he tried to open the coffin lid. Nothing happened. He hit the coffin again, harder this time.

"I think it will open now," he said.

The professor tried again to open the lid. Nothing happened at first. And then slowly, he pulled the lid open.

Dr Bloodclott gasped. He could see everything clearly because the sun was shining into the grave. Veronica was lying in the coffin. She was dressed in a white night-gown. And she was as beautiful as she had been when she was alive.

"Pass me the stick and the hammer," said the professor.

Dr Bloodclott passed him the two things.

Professor Dateman put the pointed end of the stick to the girl's heart. He kept hold of the stick with his left hand and held the hammer in his right hand. He hit the top of the stick with the hammer. Once, twice, three times. The point of the stick went into the girl's heart.

Dr Bloodclott saw all this. He saw the stick go in. He saw the girl's eyes open. He heard the girl scream. And he saw the blood coming out of her heart.

Professor Dateman pulled the stick out of Veronica's body. He climbed out of the grave.

"She's dead now. Really dead," he said.

The two men watched as the body lost its colour. The soft skin became wrinkled. And a terrible smell started coming from the grave.

"Come on. Let's put the earth back," said the professor.

The two men shovelled the earth back into the grave. Then they had a rest.

"What do we do now?" asked the doctor.

"Now we have to find Count Suckchops' grave. And do the same," answered the professor.

The two men walked around the graveyard, looking at the graves. But it was hard work. Most of the gravestones were very old, and it was difficult to read the names. After two hours they stopped.

"We'll never find the count's grave like this," said the professor.

The two men returned to the professor's house. They talked about the situation.

"What are we going to do?" asked the doctor.

"Well, I'm going to see Major Silversword. Perhaps he knows where the count is buried."

Professor Dateman phoned Major Silversword the following day. The major did not know where the count was buried. But there were a lot of books in the library of the Black Castle. Perhaps they could get the information from one of the books.

The professor met the major at the Black Castle that afternoon. They looked through many old books but did not find the information they wanted.

"I have decided to come back to the Black Castle," said the major. "I can't stay with my friends for ever."

"Are you sure you are doing the right thing?" asked the professor.

"I don't really know. But this is my home. And I don't want to live anywhere else."

"What about Madeline?"

"Madeline's getting better, thank God. But she has to stay in hospital for another few weeks. I hope that we can do something about the vampire before she comes home."

The professor thought for a few moments.

"Do you mind if I come and stay with you? I think I can help."

"Not at all. I'd like that," answered the major.

Major and Mrs Silversword and the servants returned to the Black Castle the following day. Professor Dateman was already there.

"Now, listen carefully," the professor told everybody. "I want everyone to follow my instructions.

"A vampire is frightened of two things: a cross and garlic. So everyone must have a cross on his bedroom wall, over the bed. And there must be garlic in every bedroom, over the windows and doors. If you do this, you will be safe from the vampire. Do you all understand?"

Everybody nodded.

The servants started work immediately. They put crosses on the walls in all the bedrooms. They bought garlic, and hung it over every door and window in the house. Finally everything was ready.

That night, everyone was frightened when he went to bed. But nothing happened. The vampire did not appear. Nothing happened during the next few days. But Professor Dateman and the major were not satisfied. They knew they had to kill the vampire.

During the day, the two men went round the graveyard. They opened grave after grave, but could not find the vampire. It was hard work but they had to go on.

One day the professor went to the railway station. He came back an hour later with a young woman.

"This is Susan," said the professor. "She has been travelling around the world for two years, and she has just come back. She says she can help. Do you mind if she stays with us?"

"Of course not. She is very welcome," said the major.

Susan was given the bedroom next to Madeline's.

Nothing important happened during the next two weeks. Every day the major and the professor opened five or six graves. But they did not find the vampire.

Then one morning, when the servant brought Susan's breakfast into her bedroom, he noticed something strange. The bedroom window was open and the curtains were blowing in the wind.

The servant looked over at the bed. Susan was still asleep. He looked at the wall, above the bed. The wooden cross was not there! Where was it? He looked round the room. There it was, on the floor at the other side of the bed. It was broken.

He put the breakfast tray down and quickly ran out of the room.

Two minutes later, Major Silversword and Professor Dateman came into the bedroom. The professor went over to the bed. He touched the sleeping woman on the forehead.

"Wake up, Susan," he said. "Wake up."

Susan opened her eyes.

"Are you all right?" asked the professor. "You look very pale."

Susan tried to sit up in bed, but she was too weak.

"You are not all right, are you?" said the professor.

"I . . . . " Susan stopped. The professor was looking at her in a strange way. He had noticed something. There were two small marks on Susan's neck.

Dr Bloodclott was sent for. He arrived half an hour later and examined Susan.

"There's no doubt about it," said the doctor. "You've been bitten by the vampire. We must get you into hospital immediately."

"It's too late, doctor," said Susan weakly.

Susan was rushed into hospital. She was given a blood transfusion but it was too late. She died the next day.

Professor Dateman was heart-broken. He blamed himself for Susan's death.

"It's all my fault," he said. "Why did I ever bring her to the Black Castle?"

The major sympathized with the professor. He knew exactly how the professor felt.

"Don't blame yourself," said the major. "Come on. We have work to do. We have to kill this vampire. If we don't, more people will die."

"But how can we find the grave?" asked the professor.

"I'm going to look again in the library," said the major. "There must be some information in one of the old books."

Major Silversword spent a long time in the library. Finally he came out, holding a book. He looked very excited.

"I've got it," he said. "I've found the information we need." He pointed to a page in the book.

"Look at this. Count Suckchops wasn't buried in the graveyard. His body was placed in a tomb inside the chapel."

"Come on, then. We haven't any time to waste," said the professor.

The major went back into the library and came out with a big iron key.

"I think this may be the key to the chapel door," he said. "I found it in one of the drawers in the cabinet."

The two men left the house and walked through the graveyard to the chapel. They took an axe, a torch, a wooden hammer and a stick. They dropped their tools when they reached the chapel door.

"Let's try the key," said the major. He put the key in the lock. The key fitted perfectly. But when the major tried to turn it, nothing happened.

"The lock must be very rusty. It hasn't been opened for hundreds of years," said the major.

"Let me try," suggested the professor.

The professor tried. But he could not turn the key either.

"I know," said the major. "The key needs oiling. Wait here. I'll be back in two minutes."

The major ran to the house and came back with a bottle of oil. He poured some oil over the key and put the key in the lock.

"Let's see if it works now," he said.

The major, with all his strength, tried to turn the key. Nothing happened at first. Then there was a clicking sound, and the key turned in the lock.

The major stood back, and then he kicked the door with the sole of his foot. The wooden door gave way with a groan. It opened slowly.

A terrible smell came through the doorway as the two men looked inside.

"Open the door as wide as you can," said the professor. "We need as much light as possible."

The two men went inside. Their eyes soon became accustomed to the semi-darkness.

"There it is!" said the professor. He pointed to the square-shaped tomb in the corner of the chapel. "That's the count's tomb."

The two men went over to the tomb. The major shone his torch. In the light of the torch, the two men could see the writing on the side of the tomb.

COUNT GREGORY SUCKCHOPS
1548-1606

The professor and the major examined the tomb. It was made of stone.

"How do we get it open?" asked the major.

"We'll have to slide the top off," said the professor. He touched the top of the tomb.

"The top has been fixed on with cement. If we break the cement, we will be able to push the top off."

The professor picked up the axe. He swung the axe and hit the cement, which was around the top of the tomb. Once, twice, three times. The cement cracked in several places.

The professor stopped for a rest. Then he started again. The broken cement was falling off, piece by piece.

"I think the top will come off now," he said. He put the axe down. "Come on. Push."

The two men put their hands on top of the tomb. They pushed with all their strength. Slowly, very slowly, the top started moving. Soon there was a small opening. Then the opening became bigger. The two men pushed harder. The top was hanging over the side now. With a final effort, they pushed again. The top fell over the side and landed on the floor with a loud crash.

The professor and the major looked into the tomb. They could see the coffin clearly.

Quickly the professor climbed into the tomb. He opened the coffin lid. The two men gasped. They had expected to see the sleeping vampire. But all they saw was a decaying body. The skin over the body was green and wrinkled. The eyes were open, staring upwards. The mouth was hanging open, showing long, yellow teeth.

Professor Dateman remembered how Veronica had looked when he opened her coffin. She had looked beautiful and fresh,

almost like an angel. But this was different. This was horrible.

"I don't understand this," said the professor. "This vampire is already dead."

The major did not say anything. He did not know what to say.

"But we had better make sure," the professor continued. "Pass me the stick and the hammer."

The major handed the stick and the wooden hammer to the professor. The professor put the pointed end of the stick to the vampire's heart. He hit the top of the stick twice with the hammer. The stick went into the body. But it was not necessary. The vampire was already dead. It had been dead for some days.

"I just don't understand," said the major, when the two men were back at the house.

"Neither do I," said the professor.

Susan's funeral took place the following day. Dr Bloodclott, Dr Lookall, the major and the professor were the only people who were there.

"It's a pity that Susan had to be the vampire's last victim," said the professor.

Dr Bloodclott and Dr Lookall looked at each other.

"Erm . . . . ," Dr Bloodclott began, "Susan didn't die because of the vampire. She . . . . she died of something else."

"Yes, that's right," said Dr Lookall to Professor Dateman. "You remember when Susan came here? You said that she had been travelling around the world."

The professor nodded.

"Well," Dr Lookall went on. "She knew she was going to die. That's why she came back home. You see, she was suffering from aquired immunity deficiency syndrome."

"She was suffering from what?" asked the professor.

"From AIDS, the new killer blood disease. The epidemic that has appeared during the last few years.

"So you see," continued Dr Lookall, "the vampire did not kill Susan. Susan killed the vampire."